The Story of Santa Claus

The Story of Santa Claus

By Scribbler Elf

Illustrated by the Elves

Ariel Books

Turner Publishing, Inc.

ATLANTA

Published by Turner Publishing, Inc.
A Subsidiary of Turner Broadcasting System, Inc.
1050 Techwood Drive, N.W.
Atlanta, Georgia 30318

First Edition
10 9 8 7 6 5 4 3 2 1

Acknowledgment
From *The Night Before Christmas* by Clement C. Moore, illustrated by
Scott Gustafson. Copyright © 1985 by The Tempest Company.
Reprinted by permission of Alfred A. Knopf, Inc.

Produced by Ariel Books
Art direction by Armand Eisen
Design by Maura Fadden Rosenthal
Design consulting by Michael Walsh
Production by Nancy Robins

Cover illustration © 1993 by Scott Gustafson
Frontispiece by Scott Gustafson

The Story of Santa Claus by Tim Paulson, Armand Eisen,
Megan Liberman, and Della Rowland

ISBN: 1-878685-45-7

Library of Congress Catalog Card Number: 93-60270

Distributed by Andrews and McMeel
A Universal Press Syndicate Company
4900 Main Street
Kansas City, Missouri 64112

Foreword

How do reindeer fly? Are elves invisible? Why do you live at the North Pole? How do all the presents fit into your sleigh? Do you ever get lost?

Curious children from all over the world write me letters by the thousands asking these questions and many, many more. For years I have longed to answer each letter and tell every boy and girl our story. But I'm a toymaker, not a storyteller, so nothing was done about it — until one night. As I was reading some of the children's notes to Mrs. Claus, she said, "Nicholas, we really have to get our story told, so why don't we ask Scribbler Elf to write it?" "My dear," I said, "what a jolly idea! I'll go talk to him right away." And I did! And that's how this book came about.

Scribbler Elf is our scribe. Writing is what he does best, and as you will see, he does it very well, indeed. He divides his time between the Card and Book Workshop, where he's famous for his calligraphy and verses, and the Christmas Land Archives. That's where we keep all our records: your letters, the legends, our maps, blueprints, drawings — everything! It's no small feat keeping all that information in order, but Scribbler has been with me from the beginning and has never forgotten a thing. So, who better to have written this tale?

What's more, Scribbler understood perfectly when I reminded him that the most important part of our story would be the hardest to capture in words. It's the part that you bring with you as you sit down with this book and open yourself to the magic that is Christmas. It's the magic of love that is born in the heart and can transform the entire world.

—Santa Claus

Introduction

You may have never heard of me but I'm pretty famous here at the North Pole, what with my special talents for writing and all. That's why Santa asked me to tell the true story of Santa Claus. He asked me to do it, you see, because I'm already his scribe, which means I write things down anyway. That's why they call me Scribbler Elf. I can always be found scribbling away at my desk at the Card and Book Workshop or hunched over a bunch of papers in the Christmas Land Archives.

The Archives — what a place that is! That's where we keep all of our records. We have all the letters we've ever received from you boys and girls, legends about Santa we've collected from around the world, maps of Santa's Christmas Eve routes and of spots we've explored here at the North Pole, blueprints of our little village, the family trees of all the elves who live here, not to mention the names of the animals who live with us and drawings and paintings and…well, you can imagine how much stuff there is! I spent so much time in the Archives working on this story that Santa suggested I might as well move right in — hang my hammock between a couple of storage shelves and call it home!

Before I go any further, I have to tell you, because it's so very important to Santa, that this is not just the story of Nicholas and Mrs. Claus, but the story of the Christmas spirit and what can happen when that spirit takes hold of you. How the Clauses came to live at the North Pole, how they met me and the other elves, how reindeer fly, how Santa makes it around the world in a single night — I'll tell you how all these things came about and how they happen. But more important than *how*, I'll tell you *why*. It is, of course, the magic of the spirit of Christmas.

So here it is, the real story. From Santa and Mrs. Claus, from the Archives, and from the elves — every one contributed. Not one elf passed up the chance to sit by my desk and remember out loud the happy times we've had here in Christmas Land. Oh, if I had included everything they told me this book would be fatter than 20 phone books! Lucky for me,

Mrs. Claus (bless her rosy red cheeks) helped me sort through it all and check the facts until I got the story just right.

Turning my words into pictures was a task for our very best artists. You can see the unique style of each elf. Some painted from memory — the happy memories of our wondrous journey to the North Pole and the early days of our settlement here. Some took their easels right into the bakery, post office, or toy shop and caught the busy elves at work. And some, in mufflers and mittens, bravely stuck their easels into a clump of snow and painted outside. They had to be quick to sketch the animals, what with the reindeer flying up and down and showering snow all over, and the seals and the penguins slipping and sliding all about, knocking into their easels and causing havoc. When Mrs. Claus, who keeps a kind and watchful eye on all of us, thought the artists had been out in the cold too long, she insisted they come inside, cozy up to the fire, and down some hot chocolate — her own special recipe, thick and rich and delicious.

So cozy up yourself and listen to *The Story of Santa Claus*. And remember what Santa told me — the spirit of Christmas, that magic born in the heart — that's the *real* story.

Scribbler Elf

nce upon a time in the city of Amsterdam, there lived a toymaker named Nicholas Claus. He and his wife had a snug little home with three rooms and a workshop, where Nicholas made beautiful toys and Mrs. Claus sewed clothes for the puppets and dolls. Even though they both worked very hard, they were quite poor, for few people in Amsterdam bought toys from them for their children except at Christmas. Nevertheless, the Clauses had each other, and that made them feel very rich indeed! One chilly winter afternoon, Nicholas learned exactly how rich he was. It was just a few weeks before Christmas, and . . .

Nicholas was making his way home with a bundle of pine sticks to carve into toy soldiers. Christmas was always the time of year when mothers and fathers bought nice gifts for their children, and Nicholas's head was full of ideas for new toys. As he walked along admiring the decorated shop windows, his eyes twinkled, as they always did when he was happy.

Turning a corner, Nicholas saw a ragged little boy staring into the window of a toy store. Inside the window was a brightly painted toy soldier. It had movable arms, and one hand held a little silver sword raised high. On its head was a tall blue hat with gold braid. The boy could not take his eyes off the beautiful toy.

Nicholas could tell by the child's smudged face, tattered clothes,
and dirty red stockings that he was an orphan who lived in the streets.
"No one will buy that little fellow a Christmas present this year — or any
other year," Nicholas thought sadly. As he walked on in the gathering
dark, he could not forget the expression of longing in the poor boy's face.

Suddenly he stopped in the middle of the street. "That boy *will*
have a soldier!" he exclaimed. "I'll make it for him!"

ate Christmas Eve night, Nicholas
held a toy soldier up to the candlelight in his
workshop. It was the best he had ever
made! He bundled himself up and set out
across town with the toy under his arm.
Soon he stood before a deserted building in
which he knew some street urchins slept at
night. Nicholas peered through the window.
Sure enough, there was the boy he'd seen,
huddled with several other poor youngsters
in front of a smoky fireplace.

For a moment Nicholas didn't know
what to do next. He finally decided he
would keep his identity unknown so the boy
could believe that the toy had appeared by
some Christmas magic. He waited outside
until all the boys were fast asleep, then he
crept into the building. Hanging above the
hearth to dry were the red stockings he had
seen the little boy wearing. He slipped the
soldier into one sock, making sure its blue
hat was showing.

Back outside, Nicholas watched through the window as the boy stirred with the morning light, then sat up. He was still yawning when he noticed the blue hat. Jumping up, the boy drew the soldier from the stocking. His eyes grew wide as he turned it over in his hands. Suddenly he realized that someone had left the splendid toy for him and shouted in astonishment!

This woke the other boys, who threw off their thin blankets to come see the soldier. "Who was the saint who left this wonderful toy?" they cried. No one had ever given any of them *anything*.

As he saw the joy that swept over the grimy faces of the orphan boys, Nicholas knew he had found his calling. Next year, he decided, he would make a special gift for each of the boys.

"No!" he thought. "Next year, I will make a toy for *every* poor child in Amsterdam!" And his eyes twinkled at the thought!

For many years afterward, Nicholas devoted himself to creating enough toys so that every needy child in Amsterdam would have a Christmas gift. Over time, his hair and beard had grown as white as snow, but his eyes still twinkled as brightly as ever. Mrs. Claus still helped Nicholas with the toys, but she also took in knitting and mending to make ends meet.

Although the Clauses' work made them happier than they had ever been, Nicholas was uncomfortable that more and more he was being credited for his good deeds. While the townsfolk had once referred to an "unknown saint" who brought poor children toys, people now spoke openly of Nicholas's generosity and called out to him, "Hello, Saint Nicholas!" or "Good day, Santa Claus."

Even though he was glad to be appreciated, Nicholas wanted people to think of Christmas itself, not of him, when they opened their gifts. And so he and Mrs. Claus decided to leave Amsterdam.

But the toymaker had another reason for moving on. He wanted to make more toys for still more children — all the children in the world! And there simply was not room in his modest cottage to do that.

The Clauses decided to move where no one else lived, where they could have all the space they needed. So, one hazy, winter day, they packed their few belongings into a wagon, said goodbye to Amsterdam, and headed north.

As the Clauses traveled farther and farther north, the wind got colder and colder. Frost clung to Nicholas's great white beard and covered Mrs. Claus's coat and shawl. After a few days' journey their old mare could barely stumble forward. One evening, a furious blizzard suddenly descended. The Clauses were lost in a white wall of swirling snow. Stopping the wagon, Nicholas looked at his wife in despair. "Perhaps my idea is not such a good one after all," he cried. "Perhaps this is the end!"

Mrs. Claus grasped his hand. "We'll find a way."

As they sat there waiting out the storm, they heard a whimpering sound. Climbing down from the wagon, Nicholas found lying beneath a bush a baby reindeer with an injured leg. While Mrs. Claus held the little hurt creature in her lap, Nicholas used his toymaking skills to fashion a splint. As he tenderly bandaged the tiny leg, Mrs. Claus saw how his face had brightened.

"I'm going to call the deer Twinkle," she told him, "because it has brought back the twinkle in your eyes."

DALTON BOOKSELLER #1   TRAVERSE CITY, MI
6-929-0775
   1161.02.10   12/16/95   18.12   29418

1-878685-45-7   19.95
                    SUBTOTAL   19.95
                    SALES TAX   1.20
                    TOTAL   21.15
                    CASH   21.15

J WOULD SAVE   2.00
'H BOOK$AVERS! JOIN TODAY!

------------ THANK YOU ------------

The two of them were so concerned about helping the baby
deer that, for a few moments, they forgot about their own bad
luck. They didn't even notice several colorfully clad figures
watching them from behind some trees.

They were laying Twinkle in the back of the wagon and wondering
what to do next when the men came forward. One of them introduced
himself. "My name is Erik," he said. "May I inquire what has brought
you good folks to Lapland? People rarely visit so far north."

The toymaker explained that they were looking for a place far from
people and cities, where he could build toys for all the world's children.
The Laplanders listened carefully as Nicholas described his dream, then they
looked at one another and nodded. "Perhaps we can help you," said Erik.

Without another word, one of the Lapps picked up Twinkle and the
others unharnessed the Clauses' exhausted horse and began pulling the wagon
toward a nearby clearing.

As suddenly as it had begun, the blizzard stopped. Inside the clearing, the fresh snow glowed silvery blue in the moonlight. The Lapps began making a fire, and when it was blazing, Erik motioned the Clauses to sit near it. "The place to go to fulfill your dreams is the North Pole," he told Nicholas. "There you will have all the space you need to make your toys. And we will help you get there." Then, at his whistle, several reindeer pranced into the clearing and began leaping about. Suddenly they soared right up into the cold night air! The Clauses could not believe their eyes!

"Yes," said Erik, "these reindeer — as well as the little one you took care of — belong to a very special herd. They can fly. We have chosen eight of the strongest and fastest to take you to the North Pole."

Nicholas's eyes twinkled as he looked at the reindeer. "Well, well," he chuckled. "Flying reindeer! My friend, I am grateful to you, indeed. But how will they help me get to the North Pole? My *wagon* does not fly!"

"Never mind your wagon," Erik smiled. "We have another gift for you. Wait here!" And he disappeared through the snowy boughs of the trees.

In a short while, Erik returned with an old man. He was bent into the shape of a question mark, with a beard even longer than Nicholas's and almost as white. His ancient face was craggy and seamed, but his eyes blazed. Erik guided him to the fire, where he sat down and spoke to Nicholas.

"I am Karl, the king of the Laplanders," the aged man said, "and Erik has told me of your dream for the children of the world. We can help you." The king of the Lapps waved his hand. "The sleigh!" he called.

At that, eight flying reindeer landed soundlessly in the clearing. They were pulling a beautiful sleigh. "This sleigh is yours to use in your mission," Karl told Nicholas. "And these are your reindeer — Donner, Blitzen, Dasher, Dancer, Vixen, Prancer, Comet, and Cupid." At the sound of its name, each proud reindeer pawed the snow with a cloven hoof.

"This sleigh is very special, and I will tell you its story," continued Karl. "Long, long ago, during the reign of King Olaf the Kind, a harsh, endless winter beset our land. This unbroken frozen night drove the joy from everyone's heart. Many simply gave up trying to find food and firewood, and they perished. King Olaf feared most for the children during this terrible time. So at Christmas, he ordered his sleigh — this sleigh — to be filled with food and clothing and trinkets for the children. Then he set out to visit his subjects, swearing he would not rest until he knew all were fed and warm. By a miracle, the sleigh whisked King

Olaf to every corner of his kingdom in a single night. And though it is not a large sleigh, somehow there was always enough in it to feed and clothe every child in Lapland.

"The secret of the sleigh is not simply magic, but love. Its magic works only when the sleigh is used with a loving spirit. Since the time of King Olaf, we have been waiting for someone with just such a spirit. You are that one, Nicholas. Use the sleigh with our blessing. And do not be afraid that people will forget the spirit of Christmas and think only of you when they receive your gifts, for you *are* the Spirit of Christmas. Hereafter you shall be known as the saint that you are, and the world will call you *Santa Claus*."

That night, the Lapps prepared a magnificent supper for their new friends from afar. Believing now that their dream was possible after all, the Clauses fell into a contented sleep after supper and awoke with the dawn to make an early start for the North Pole. Santa called out his reindeers' names. At the sound of his voice, they shook the snow from their backs and rose, ready to go!

The generous Lapps gave the Clauses food to take with them and warm boots and two bright red snowsuits with fur trim. "We'll see you again," promised Karl as Santa and Mrs. Claus stepped into the sleigh. "In the meantime," he laughed, "these red suits will make you easier to find in a blizzard!" Santa joined him with a deep "HO, HO, HO!" Then he waved his hand, and the sleigh leapt skyward.

itting comfortably in their new sleigh, the Clauses headed north once again. At the end of the day, Santa spotted a snowy glade near the edge of a forest, where he brought the sleigh down. (His first landing was a bit rough and raised quite a cloud of snow, but, of course, he's a master driver now!) After the snow had settled, Santa noticed several elves peering from behind the trees. "Hello there," he called out — at which point they all disappeared!

A moment later, one came out again and stood near the sleigh. "I am Driana," she said. "We elves are surprised you can see us, since we are not visible to humans. But because you can see us, you must live by magic, as we do. And so we welcome you to our forest. Look carefully, and you will see our homes."

Sure enough, high in the trees above, the Clauses could see colorful little elf dwellings — some round, some shaped like tops and stars, and some like tiny human cottages.

"Come," said Driana. "We will make you a place to spend the night, and I will tell you about the time when elves and humans lived together."

As they settled around the campfire, Driana began her tale. "Ages and ages ago," she said, "we elves lived in the land from which you came. In that time, humans lived together with the elves in the great woods. They, too, understood the language of the forest and the beasts who inhabited it. They could speak with the spirits in the babbling brooks, the spreading oaks, the ancient stones, and the blooming marigolds. When the world was bathed in the magic light of the moon at midnight, elves and men would join hands in a starlit clearing and dance until dawn amid the tinkling laughter of sprites and pixies.

"But humans changed. There were those who believed magic to be evil. Gradually they convinced others. Their hearts, once filled with the joy of magic and mystery, became fearful. They became convinced that riches would save them from their fears. Magic faded from that part of the world, like the light of the sun fades at the end of the day. People lost the knack of speaking to the animals. They cut down the forests to build villages, using the woodworking skills we elves had taught them. They banded together and ceased to come out at night to dance with us. Eventually, they could not even see us.

"We missed the humans, but we knew our time among them had passed, and as their towns and cities became more numerous, we moved ever northward. And the magic has come with us."

After listening to the story of the elves, Santa told them of his own past. Under the dancing Northern Lights, he explained his dream of finding a place where he could make toys for all the world's children. Then he asked if the elves would help him, for he knew they were masters at woodworking.

"You spoke of the Christmas Spirit," said a young elf who knew quite a number of spirits but never had heard of this one. "Could you tell us about it?"

"Yes, I think I can," Santa said. Then he told the elves about that Christmas long ago when he made a toy soldier for an orphan boy in Amsterdam. He described how he felt when he saw the boys' faces as they stared at the wonderful gift. Then Santa pointed to the North Star. "Let us follow the North Star to the place where we can all work together to give every child that feeling of being special — the feeling of being loved."

At that moment, something marvelous happened. The North Star flickered. It bathed Santa in a halo of light that disappeared in an instant. And from then on (although no one knew it yet), none of them would grow any older — they would stay just as they were forever.

Now, the elves were used to magic, but this was the first Christmas Magic they had ever seen. With this sign, they knew that Santa's dream was a truly special mission, and they all pledged to accompany him.

"We will always remember this night," Santa said. "In years to come we will light a great Yule Log, like the mighty logs in this fire, to remind us of the night that starlight came to earth."

The next morning, the elves were packed and ready to go before Santa had even harnessed the reindeer. The jolly company continued north until they reached the Great Northern Sea. "How will we get across?" asked the elves. "There are far too many of us to fly in the sleigh."

Santa sat down to think. Ever since the North Star had shone down on him, Santa seemed to glow. Now, even when he was deep in thought, his eyes twinkled like stars, his smile beamed like the sun, and his cheeks blazed like two bright red fires. Attracted by the unusual light, walruses, polar bears, seals, and penguins began swimming toward Santa. Soon the animals were nuzzling Santa, licking his face and hands.

"I have it!" exclaimed Santa. "We'll cross the sea on ice floes, and our new friends here will guide us." The elves agreed that this was an excellent idea, so they piled their belongings onto the floating ice and pushed off. "North Pole, here we come!" they cheered.

With the seals and penguins leading the way and the polar bears and walruses pushing behind, Santa and his crew paddled their ice floes across the Great Northern Sea. When the reindeer flying above began to whinny, they knew they were getting close to their destination. At last, an ice plain came into view, and before long they were scrambling onto the snowy shore of the North Pole.

They had made it!

An awed silence fell upon them. They took off their hats (if they had them) and listened to the faint humming of the wind at the top of the world. Then they cheered. It was a cheer such as had never been heard in that quiet place. And when it ended, it seemed that its echo would never stop.

The elves set about making camp, and after supper they drifted off into a dream-filled sleep. But not Santa. By the light of an elfin lamp, he immediately began making plans to build a little city — with houses, a reindeer stable, a bakery, a post office, and, of course, a toy factory.

"I will call my dream city Christmas Land," he decided.

NORTH POLE

Reindeer Barn

Toy Factory

Santa's House

Elves' House

Bakery

Post Office

With the help of the Master Builder Elf, Santa's plan for Christmas Land was drawn up the next day. And since no one saw any reason to wait, they began building right away. After all, Christmas would be there before they knew it, and Santa was determined to fulfill his dream this year.

Lo and behold, the Laplanders arrived that very day to help! They even brought sleds loaded with wood and other materials they knew would be in short supply at the Pole.

Everyone had a task — even the animals did their part (except for the seals, who were so excited they just got in the way). Crews worked around the clock, and in just a few weeks the elves had completed the finishing touches.

One little elf child had sat quietly amid the flurry of building activity. When Santa asked her what was wrong, she told him she missed the trees in her old forest home. "Then you shall have a tree," Santa promised her.

No sooner had the last nail been hammered than Santa called a meeting in the town square.

"Dear citizens of the North Pole," Santa began, "you have built a beautiful city here!" Everyone smiled proudly and clapped one another on the back. "And now," Santa went on, "as the finishing touch to our new home, we are going to find our first Christmas Tree!"

No one was happier than the little elf. But where would they find a tree at the North Pole? Santa had a plan for that, too.

He released one of the doves the elves had brought with them from the forest. "Come, bring a sleigh," Santa said. "We'll follow this bird."

And they did, for many miles, until they came to an immense valley. There below was a forest of tall Noble Firs. The little elf hugged Santa around the neck, and the other elves had to admit that they, too, were happy to see trees again. They watched as the dove perched on the tallest and most beautiful of the firs. Its lofty snow-covered limbs were frosted pinkish white by the late-afternoon sun that was just dipping behind the hills. The little party slid down the mountain slope and gathered in a ring around the magnificent tree.

Joining hands around the Noble Fir, the little people sang their old elfin
songs. Then Santa taught them some Christmas carols, and they sang those,
too, until it grew late and it was time to go home. As they loaded their
wonderful tree on the sleigh and began hauling it home, Santa taught the
elves a carol about a Christmas Tree! Here is how it went:

O CHRISTMAS TREE!

O Christmas Tree, O Christmas Tree!
How lovely are thy branches!
O Christmas Tree, O Christmas Tree!
How lovely are thy branches!
Not only green in summer's heat,
But also winter's snow and sleet.
O Christmas Tree, O Christmas Tree!
How lovely are thy branches!

O Christmas Tree, O Christmas Tree!
Thy candles shine out brightly!
O Christmas Tree, O Christmas Tree!
Thy candles shine out brightly!
Each bough doth hold its tiny light
That makes each toy to sparkle bright.
O Christmas Tree, O Christmas Tree!
Thy candles shine out brightly!

The First Christmas at the North Pole had begun! Later, Santa
and the elves planted more saplings where they had found the Noble Firs,
so that every year they could select the tallest and straightest of these trees to
display in the town square, which they named Christmas Tree Square.

While Santa's expedition was looking for a tree, Mrs. Claus and the rest of the elves were busy making decorations for it. The elves wanted the Christmas Tree to remind them of their old forest home, so they created ornaments that looked like their brightly colored treehouses. The next morning, after the Noble Fir was placed in the square, and all the elves had hung their ornaments on it, the little reindeer Twinkle added the crowning touch to the very tip top — a gold star!

And that is what they still do, every Christmas, even to this day!

Decorating the first Christmas Tree was like a festival for the elves, and when the tree was finished they continued to frolic in the snow. For the rest of that day they ice-skated, went down a giant ice slide, had snowball fights, and played tag with the reindeer.

Santa was right: the Christmas Tree had made the elves feel right at home in the North Pole. That night, worn out from all the decorating and frolicking, they tucked into their hammocks and beds and slept as soundly as they had in the forest. The tinkling sound of their snoring jingled and jangled the timbers of Elf House as the elves dreamed of the wonderful toys they would make for the children of the world.

uring that first Christmas at the North Pole, one thing after another was taken care of, and somehow everything got done in time. As the years went by, the elves and the Clauses got better at scheduling things. Now Christmas Land runs like clockwork! Here's what happens every year.

The Christmas Tree is chosen twelve days before Christmas. During the twelve days that follow, there is much to do. All year the elves have been making toys. Now the final touches must be applied and everything wrapped. Letters from children must be read. Santa's route must be planned. The sleigh must be polished. But first . . . the Christmas Cleaning must be done!

In case you didn't know it, elves are first-class housekeepers, and the Christmas Cleaning is where they really shine! They mop and scrub and wax and buff and sweep the stairs and shake the rugs and dust the banisters and polish the brass and wash the linens. Smells of fresh wax and clean laundry waft through Elf House as brooms and mops and feather dusters whisk into every corner. Everything must be spick-and-span for the North Pole's biggest day!

As you can imagine, the North Pole Post Office is a very busy place at Christmas. Special requests from children all over the world must be carefully sorted and delivered to Santa.

Sometimes the Post Office becomes a blizzard of letters, and it is all everyone can do to see that nothing gets lost. One Christmas the letters piled up so high that a sneeze caused an avalanche that buried the Postmaster Elf completely! Guided by his squeals, the helper elves worked a whole day to dig him out.

Of course, no one is busier at Christmas than Santa Claus. But, somehow, he always finds time to do everything that has to be done, especially
one of his favorite Christmas jobs — reading the letters he receives from
children.

Sometimes children ask for a great deal of things, making their letters
very long, but Santa goes over each and every one. He loves to read them
aloud to Mrs. Claus, and she loves to watch his eyes twinkle as he does so.

Even Santa can't make enough dolls, trains, soldiers, and teddy bears for all the children in the world by himself. He needs lots of helpers. But he makes sure the toys from his North Pole Toy Factory are as splendid and as fun to play with as those he made in Amsterdam. How? By playing with them!

Santa calls this "testing," but Mrs. Claus knows better. "You never grew up, Nicholas," she laughs, when he comes home carrying a toy or two.

Then he explains what's special about each one. "Like snowflakes and children," he tells her, "no two toys are alike."

The North Pole Toy Factory includes the Book and Card Workshop.
There elves make all the cards that accompany the Christmas gifts. They
also write and illustrate special Christmas books — like the one you are
reading right now. In fact, their favorite subject is the story of Santa and
Christmas Land.

Would you believe that all the cookies and jelly rolls and plum tarts and cupcakes for all the world's Christmas celebrations could be made in one single night? Only the North Pole Bakery could do it! You should see the flour and sugar fly as the elves sift, measure, and stir!

Of course, nothing leaves the Bakery without the Chief Taster Elf giving it the taste test. By the end of the night, he's dizzy from all the treats he has sampled. It's a hard job, he says, but someone has to do it.

There is only one place at the North Pole that's sweeter than the Bakery, and that's the Candy Caves. The elves discovered them one day while they were prospecting. Beneath all the ice was the Chocolate Brook that gurgled up through the Rock Candy Cliffs and flowed through Sugar Valley, where the elves found lollipop flowers, gumdrop bushes, and candy cane trees growing.

The elves built the Jellybean Trail, which winds up Marzipan Mountain, and began mining the caves. The candy they harvest each year goes to children all the world over. And now you know where all your Christmas stocking candy comes from and why visions of sugar-plums dance in your head after you're tucked into your bed on Christmas Eve!

All the finished toys, cards, candies, and confections wind up in the North Pole Giftwrapping Workshop, where elves wrap each present with patterned paper and colored bows, then tie on the special hand-painted cards. The workshop is a flurry of activity, with scissors snipping, paper rustling, and ribbons twirling.

The elves must also clearly
mark the destination of each package
so that Santa can see it easily.
There's no time for hunting around
in the bag while the sleigh is perched
on a steep, snowy rooftop!

As Christmas Eve gets closer, Santa's eight reindeer get extra helpings of oats, apples, and carrots. Rupert, the Reindeer-Keeper Elf, tends to the reindeer and sometimes even sleeps in their stable as Christmas nears. It's his job to see that Santa's reindeer are ready for their all-important Christmas mission.

All year long the reindeer practice flying and landing — but mostly landing. You see, flying is easy for them, but landing is another matter, especially when they are pulling a sleigh piled high with presents. So what do they do? Practice, of course! Every day (and even after dinner), no matter what building you're in, you can hear *Thump, thump! Thump, thump!* overhead as the reindeer practice landing on all the roofs in Christmas Land.

Certain elves have the very special job of caring for Santa's sleigh, the magical gift from the king of the Lapps. Just before the Big Trip, they make sure it is in perfect condition. They wax the runners, oil the harness, polish the bells to gleaming, and plump up Santa's pillow.

Along the Christmas route, Santa makes sure that a lucky child or two will catch a glimpse of his sleigh. The delight on their faces reminds him of the faces of the little orphan boys in Amsterdam all those years ago, and this makes his eyes twinkle. Have you ever seen Santa's sleigh? Or heard it land on your roof?

On the night before Christmas Eve, the Clauses hear a ring at their door. It's the elf children, come caroling. Their high sweet voices ring out through the cold crisp night as they sing the songs they learned on that first Christmas Tree hunt long, long ago. Every Christmas since then, the youngest ones have spent this night caroling, making Santa's house their last stop. They know that Mrs. Claus has hot spiced cider waiting for them on the stove.

After the caroling, Mrs. Claus bundles Santa off to an early bedtime. Tomorrow night is his Big Trip, and he must be up early to study the route.

Christmas Eve morning for Santa begins with a long meeting with the Navigator Elf to go over this year's route. The decision of where to go first, second, third, and so on, is based on certain practical considerations —

such as the weather, how the sleigh has been loaded, and who's been naughty and nice. But mostly Santa likes to try a different route each year. It's simply more interesting — like finding a new way to walk to school. Santa doesn't worry much about taking shortcuts, because in King Olaf's magical sleigh, the trip always lasts exactly one night!

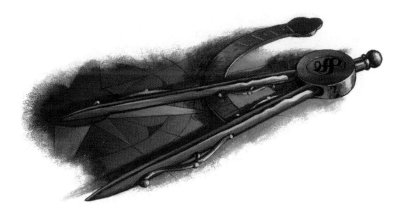

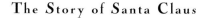

It's Christmas Eve! Time to fly! Even though Santa has made this trip many times, Mrs. Claus always worries about him. She makes sure he has checked his list *twice* and hands him his thermos of hot chocolate. Then, beneath the sprig of mistletoe that dangles from a beam in the Sleigh Coach House, she kisses him for luck. For a moment they look into each other's eyes, and Santa's are twinkling like the North Star.

Santa's Christmas ride was described in a famous poem called "The Night Before Christmas." The elves made a book of the poem, and when Santa is out of sight, Mrs. Claus reads the book to the very young elves — just as someone is going to read it to you right now!

The Night Before Christmas

by

Clement C. Moore

'Twas the night before Christmas, when all through the house
Not a creature was stirring, not even a mouse.
The stockings were hung by the chimney with care,
In hopes that St. Nicholas soon would be there.
The children were nestled all snug in their beds,
While visions of sugarplums danced in their heads.

And Mama in her kerchief, and I in my cap,
Had just settled our brains for a long winter's nap,
When out on the lawn there arose such a clatter,
I sprang from my bed to see what was the matter.
Away to the window I flew like a flash,
Tore open the shutters and threw up the sash.
The moon on the breast of the new-fallen snow
Gave a luster of midday to objects below,
When what to my wondering eyes should appear,
But a miniature sleigh and eight tiny reindeer,
With a little old driver, so lively and quick,
I knew in a moment it must be St. Nick.

More rapid than eagles his coursers they came,
And he whistled and shouted and called them by name:
"Now, Dasher! Now, Dancer! Now, Prancer and Vixen!
On, Comet! On, Cupid! On, Donder and Blitzen!
To the top of the porch! To the top of the wall!
Now dash away! Dash away! Dash away all!"
As dry leaves that before the wild hurricane fly,
When they meet with an obstacle, mount to the sky,
So up to the housetop the coursers they flew,
With a sleigh full of toys, and St. Nicholas, too.

And then, in a twinkling, I heard on the roof
The prancing and pawing of each little hoof.
As I drew in my head and was turning around,
Down the chimney St. Nicholas came with a bound.
He was dressed all in fur, from his head to his foot,
And his clothes were all covered with ashes and soot;
A bundle of toys he had flung on his back,
And he looked like a peddler just opening his pack.
His eyes how they twinkled! His dimples, how merry!
His cheeks were like roses, his nose like a cherry!
His droll little mouth was drawn up like a bow,
And the beard on his chin was as white as the snow.
The stump of a pipe he held tight in his teeth,
And the smoke it encircled his head like a wreath.
He had a broad face and a little round belly
That shook, when he laughed, like a bowlful of jelly.
He was chubby and plump, a right jolly old elf,
And I laughed when I saw him, in spite of myself.

A wink of his eye and a twist of his head,
Soon gave me to know I had nothing to dread.
He spoke not a word, but went straight to his work,
And filled all the stockings, then turned with a jerk.
And laying his finger aside of his nose,
And giving a nod, up the chimney he rose.

He sprang to his sleigh, to his team gave a whistle,
And away they all flew like the down of a thistle.
But I heard him exclaim, ere he drove out of sight,
"Happy Christmas to all, and to all a good night!"

Back at the North Pole, Santa lands his empty sled in Christmas Tree Square, where the elves are waiting to cheer him in. Stepping out of the sleigh, he pats each of his reindeer and tells his loyal crew, "Thanks to you, we gave the whole world Christmas! And what a Christmas!"

Then Santa *always* climbs into a hot bath, for Mrs. Claus *always* has one steaming when he comes in the door. "Ahhh," Santa says as he soaks his tired bones. And while he takes a much-needed nap, the others prepare for Christmas at the North Pole!

Now that the rest of the world has had its Christmas, those at the North Pole will celebrate, starting with the Great Christmas Feast! It takes a lot of food, many large pans, and even more helping hands to feed everyone there. Each elf and animal has a special job to do to help prepare the feast — even Santa! There are pies to bake, stuffing to stir, and turkeys to roast.

Before long the enormous kitchen is filled with the rich smells of yams browning, sauces bubbling, and eggnog simmering as the elves cook up Mrs. Claus's favorite Christmas recipes, which she has carefully written down in her recipe book.

Elf Wanda's Apple Dressing
(enough for about 225 hungry elves)

20 loaves of dried woodnut bread
any left-over spoon bread
7½ pounds onion
3 pounds celtic celery
7½ pounds elf butter
5 pounds sundraberry broth
1 gallon arctic sage
6 handful marjoram, oregano, blue basil, parsley
1 handful thyme, garlic, and pine needles
half a handful apples and fruit.

Chop vegetables and fruit. Saute onions and celery in
butter then add everything else ~ broth last. Use wooden
spoon to Divide dressing into greased baking dishes
and put them in oven about 20 minutes before turkey
is done. Remind the elves not to let the dressing sit out.

The Kringles' Christmas
Cranberry Relish
(Makes about 6 gallons)

5 pecks cave cranberries
17 p candy sugar
9 s hoarfrost
7 c orange juice
2 h fuls of orange
1¼ c

The large pot to use to make the relish. Put everything
best pot to use to make the relish. Put everything
in and stir till boiling, then remove kettle from
fire. The heat from the kettle will simmer the
relish. As soon as the berries pop open set the
kettle outside (covered) till the relish gets
nice and cold.

Elf Elvin's Eggnog

...quin egg yolks
...k candy sugar
...milk
...brandy
...m

...ugar, and
...tard is thick enough to coat the back
...ke sure the yolks are cooked thoroughly.
...doesn't scorch. Remove pan from
...remaining milk. Let cool and add brandy.
...cellar to chill. Just before serving, whip
...fold into cold eggnog. Sprinkle
w/ nutme...

Stir
stove
Put in
the crea...

Yulet... ...Mincemeat Pie

...10 2-crust pie
...e. They can mix
...e.

17 pounds...
several po...
apples a...
4 handfuls...
orange zes...
lemon zest...
grated nut...
a cup of ru...

Chop apples, ...ns... ...mbine everything, then scoop
into pie crust... ...with butter. Cover with top
crust and cri... ...then cut three air vents in
the top. Bake ...50 minutes at 400 degrees.

The plates have been set out, the glasses are filled, and everyone is seated. The Great Christmas Feast is about to begin! The little ones' eyes grow wide as a troop of elves carry the Christmas Turkeys to the table. As the procession moves forward, the elves sing a special carol. Then Santa raises his hand, clears his throat, and recites a Christmas poem (which goes like this):

We gather each year
With good food and cheer —
For we're proud, and I'll tell you the reason:

We give the world joy,
And each child a toy.
Now let's share our great feast of the season!

Everyone shouts "Merry Christmas!" and begins passing the
heaping bowls of food. The Great Christmas Feast commences! As
Santa serves the turkey, he gives a special word of thanks or compliment
to each elf for some large (or small) task well done. The light from
the candles flickers around the room, and great feelings of love and
togetherness fill every heart.

Christmas at Santa's house may be the last Christmas celebration of the year, but those who spend it with him say it is the best! Everyone relaxes after a job well done. Better still, they can finally open their presents! (And the surprises they come up with at the North Pole are well worth the wait!) No one is forgotten, from the youngest reindeer to the oldest elf.

The sounds of laughter, Christmas carols, and paper ripping can be heard all day and long after the night sky has turned dark blue. Then,

one by one, the lights in the elves' nursery go out as the little ones are tucked in with their new teddy bears, and humans, elves, and animals alike all settle in for a long winter's nap. Just before the last candle is snuffed, you can hear this jolly cry:

"MERRY CHRISTMAS TO ALL, AND TO ALL A GOOD NIGHT!"

The text of this book is set in Nicholas Cochin and the display in Harlem.
The text for *The Night Before Christmas* is set in Flourish, and
the title treatment in Duc De Berry and Adine Kirnberg Script.

Type was set by NK Graphics in Keene, New Hampshire.
Color separations were done by Capitol Engraving in Nashville, Tennessee.
This book was printed by Inland Press in Menomonee Falls, Wisconsin.

Interior art by Maryjane Begin, John Berkey, Richard Bernal, James Bernardin,
Krista Brauckmann, Gary Cooley, Scott Gustafson, Jim Himsworth, Victoria Lisi,
Elizabeth Miles, Robyn Officer, Wayne Parmenter, and Ruth Sanderson.